THE SHAGGY DOG

WALT DISNEY PICTURES PRESENTS

The Movie Storybook

Screenplay by The Wibberleys and Geoff Rodkey and Jack Amiel & Michael Begler

Based on "The Shaggy Dog" Screenplay by Bill Walsh and Lillie Hayward and "The Shaggy D.A." Screenplay by Don Tait

Produced by David Hoberman and Tim Allen

Directed by Brian Robbins

DISNEY PRESS

New York

Printed in the United States of America

First Edition

13 5 7 9 10 8 6 4 2

Library of Congress Control Number 2005925555

ISBN 0-7868-4862-6

In a peaceful monastery set deep within the Himalayas, a very special sheepdog joined the monks in meditation. That's right, a sheepdog. He had just settled in when a rubber ball bounced across the room and out the far door. Instantly, the sheepdog was ready to pounce. He was a special dog, but not so special that a game of fetch didn't get his tail wagging.

Excited, the dog chased after the ball, but the moment he hit the snowy slope outside, he skidded to a stop. Standing in front of him was a team of soldiers with tranquilizer guns. The dog's heart sank as he realized his mistake. The rubber ball had been nothing but a trap.

A few months later, in a courtroom in an American town, assistant district attorney Dave Douglas was first in line to become the new district attorney. His boss, Ken Hollister, was retiring in a couple of months, and Dave wanted that job. All he had to do to get it was win this case against Justin Forrester—a high school teacher who was accused of setting fire to the local Grant and Strictland Industries laboratory—and then get elected.

As far as Dave was concerned, Forrester was guilty. The teacher was an animal-rights activist who believed that the lab employees were experimenting on animals. He had even admitted to breaking into the lab to help the poor critters escape!

Grant and Strictland Industries denied that they did animal testing. This would be the easiest win of Dave's life! The only drawback? The case was keeping him away from his family—his wife, Rebecca; his son, Josh; and his daughter, Carly, who happened to be on Justin Forrester's side. Forrester was Carly's favorite teacher, and the person who inspired her to become an animal-rights activist herself. But Dave couldn't let his daughter's opinions get in his way. He made a powerful opening argument, then went outside to talk to his adoring press.

Meanwhile, at Grant and Strictland Industries, Dr. Kozak entered the lab with his boss, Lance Strictland. Sitting on a table was the kidnapped sheepdog from Tibet.

"Dogs typically age seven years for every human year," Kozak explained. "But in this one," he said, pointing to the sheepdog, "a genetic mutation reversed the equation. He *lives* seven years for every human year. This dog is over three hundred years old!"

Kozak told his boss that if they could transmit that gene to humans, then humans could live superlong lives, too. They had already injected some of the dog's cells into other animals around the lab. Some of the animals had developed doglike traits, but that had happened in the early tests. Kozak assured Strictland that those kinks had been worked out. All they had to do was keep testing the sheepdog's DNA on other animals, and sooner or later they would figure out the secret to eternal life.

Lance Strictland grinned an evil grin. Not only would he make billions of dollars off this dog, but once they had the fountain-of-youth serum, he could take it and fix his aging body. He told Kozak and the other lab workers to get back to their experiments.

Outside the lab, Carly Douglas and her boyfriend, Trey, were lying on the front sidewalk of Grant and Strictland Industries with some other protesters.

"Grant and Strictland's lying, so we're lying down!" the protesters chanted.

Dave Douglas showed up and told his daughter to go home. The news crews were there covering the protest, and she was making him look bad. But Carly stood her ground.

"I'm sorry, but as a member of the Animal Rescue Group, there are certain principles I must uphold," Carly said.

"If you don't go home, you're grounded," Dave told her.

Carly threw up her hands in frustration and dragged Trey out of there.

But Carly didn't go home. Instead, she talked Trey into breaking into the lab. If they saw animals inside, they could prove that Mr. Forrester was right!

Together, Carly and Trey entered the building by a back door. They were only inside for about five seconds when a big, beautiful sheepdog came barreling toward them. The sheepdog had broken free of the lab! He ran right past Carly and Trey and out into the sunshine.

"We did it!" Carly cheered, following the dog. "We proved Mr. Forrester right! We'll go to the media! Show them that we've got this . . . dog who's got no tags or markings . . . and that we can't actually prove came from Grant and Strictland."

Carly's shoulders slumped. This dog actually proved nothing.

"So what do we do with him?" Trey asked.

"He was wandering the freeway!" Carly lied to her mother. "If we hadn't picked him up, he could've been killed." At least that part was true.

"Awesome!" Josh cheered. "We should've gotten a dog a long time ago."

"Josh, we're not keeping him," Rebecca said. "Your father would never allow it. He hates dogs."

"Shouldn't the decision to get a household pet be made by the people who actually spend a lot of time in the household?" Carly suggested.

Rebecca looked at the dog, and Carly knew she had won. No one could turn down that adorable, furry face.

A few hours later, Dave came home.

"No! No! No!" he shouted. "This is a dog-free household!"

As much as his kids protested, Dave insisted that the dog, which they had already named Shaggy, had to go back to wherever it came from. Hearing this, Shaggy panicked and bit Dave's hand.

"Ow!" Dave cried loudly. "I'm calling the pound!"

Soon enough, an Animal Control truck was driving away with the sheepdog inside.

That night, some odd things started happening to Dave. As he worked in his home office, he noticed that his tongue kept hanging out of his mouth. He also couldn't seem to stop scratching behind his ears.

The next morning, he woke up curled into a ball at the foot of his bed. Then when he was done with his shower, he shook all the water off instead of reaching for a towel. At breakfast, his coffee tasted horrible, but he finished off his bacon in two big bites and lapped up his cereal right from the bowl!

That day in the courtroom, Dave was questioning Kozak on the stand. The other lawyer made an objection and before Dave knew what he was doing, he *growled* at her!

"Mr. Douglas, did you just *growl* at opposing counsel?" the judge asked.

"Of course not, Your Honor!" Dave answered quickly. "I just have a tickle in my throat."

But suddenly he was growling again. And again! He couldn't seem to finish a sentence without growling. Scared and confused, Dave looked at the judge.

"Can I have an, um . . . *rrrrr* . . . *rrrrrr* . . ." he tried.

"Recess?" asked the judge.

"Yes!" Dave cried.

"Ten minutes," announced the judge, looking a little disturbed.

Dave ran out of the courtroom and went directly to the dog pound. The man working behind the counter promised Dave that there was nothing wrong with Shaggy. Dave demanded to see the sheepdog.

"What did you do to me?" he asked Shaggy. "Why am I acting like this?"

All around him the other dogs barked. Dave's heart was pounding.

"Stop it!" Dave demanded, his voice like a bark itself.

And suddenly, Dave found himself on all fours. He looked down at his hands, but they were paws! Dave ran outside and caught a glimpse of himself in the window of a television store. He looked just like Shaggy! Dave had turned into a sheepdog!

"I'm a dog!" he cried, shocked. Then he turned and ran for home.

When Dave got to the front door he grabbed at the doorknob but couldn't get ahold of it with his new paws. So he pressed the doorbell with his nose. The door opened in a flash. Dave couldn't have been more relieved to see his daughter.

"Shaggy! You're back!" Carly exclaimed.

"I'm not Shaggy! I'm Dad! You've got to help me, Carly!" Dave shouted, but all that came out was a lot of barking.

"Well, aren't you talkative?" Carly said, scratching his neck.

Just then, Josh walked in. "Hey, where'd he come from?" he asked.

"Dad must have dropped him off," Carly replied.

Dave was very frustrated. He had to find a way to talk to his kids. Then he saw it—the Scrabble game on a shelf in the living room. He grabbed the box in his mouth and pulled it down, dumping out the letters. Patiently, Dave used his paw to try to spell out a sentence.

I . . . A M . . .

"Bad doggie!" Carly scolded. Then she and Josh cleaned up all the tiles, not even noticing that their dad had been trying to send them a message.

Suddenly, a car horn honked outside.

"That's Janey. I gotta go," Carly said. "I'm getting a tattoo!"

"*What?!*" Dave exclaimed. Of course, all that came out was a bark.

"I'm going to get the Animal Rescue Group logo," Carly told Josh.

Dave raced outside, barking and snarling at Janey. Scared, Janey drove away.

"What has gotten into you? Bad dog!" Carly cried.

The next thing Dave knew, Josh was taking him to the park. There, a beagle, an Akita, a Rottweiler, and a poodle all surrounded Dave.

"Have any of you ever heard of a human being turning into a dog?" Dave asked. But they didn't listen. All they wanted was to sniff him and play with him. Dave knew there was a reason he didn't like dogs!

"Shaggy! Catch!" Josh shouted, throwing a Frisbee.

"I am *not* catching the Frisbee. I need to get some information," Dave said. But the next second, instinct took over and he was hurtling through the air, jumping for the Frisbee.

"Got it!" he shouted, grabbing the plastic toy in his teeth.

Meanwhile, Gwen and Larry, two Grant and Strictland employees, had gotten the real Shaggy, the Tibetan sheepdog, back from the pound and returned him to his cage in the lab.

"Are you going to be a good boy?" Larry asked.

Shaggy shook his head "no."

"You get the cattle prod," Gwen said to Larry. "I'll get the needle."

Shaggy threw a nervous glance at the monkey in the cage across from his. This was not going to be fun. The monkey barked in agreement.

Dave the sheepdog breathed a sigh of relief when Josh brought him home, and he saw Rebecca. *She* would recognize him! He bounded right up to her and barked. Unfortunately, Rebecca just looked sullen.

"What's for dinner?" Josh asked.

"Your father's cooking," Rebecca said. "At least he was—the last time he returned one of my phone calls."

Uh-oh, Dave thought. She's mad. But what was he supposed to do? He couldn't call her back. He was a dog!

That night, Rebecca took Dave out to the garage and put out a couple of old blankets for him to sleep on.

"Sorry, Shaggy," she said. "I'd let you sleep inside, but my husband wouldn't allow it."

This is funny—not! Dave thought. "I'm sorry about tonight," he said to his wife. "I love you!"

But all that came out were more barks.

Rebecca went to bed, clearly upset that her husband wasn't home.

In the middle of the night, Dave woke up curled into a ball in the garage. He was human again! Thrilled, he ran upstairs to explain everything to Rebecca, who had dozed off.

"I know you're mad," he said. "But there's a simple—although kind of hard to swallow—explanation. I turned into a dog!"

Rebecca looked at Dave as if he had lost his mind, and tossed him right out of their room.

The next day, hoping to figure out why he had temporarily turned into a dog, Dave asked Carly where she had found Shaggy. Carly, knowing her dad would flip if he found out that she had snuck into Grant and Strictland Industries, retold her lie.

"I told you—walking on the side of the freeway . . . by the mall," she said.

Later that morning, Dave went to his doctor and explained everything that had happened to him. The doctor told him he was just overstressed. Disappointed, Dave went to the pound to see Shaggy again and found out that his owner had come to take him home. The man behind the counter couldn't remember the name of Shaggy's owner. Dave was at a loss. All he could do was hope that it was all over. Maybe he would never turn into a dog again.

In the courtroom, Dave's boss told him he had heard what happened in court the day before. Hollister wasn't happy. Dave apologized and said he had had some kind of food poisoning, but was fine now. *I hope,* Dave thought.

Soon, Forrester took the stand and Dave questioned him about the things he had seen in the Grant and Strictland lab, hoping to show the jury that Forrester was crazy.

"I admit I broke in, but I swear I didn't start that fire," Forrester said. "If you ask me, Kozak set it himself, to cover up what he's doing in that lab."

"The police didn't find any animals," Dave reminded Forrester.

"I saw what I saw!" Forrester protested. "There was a dog hooked up to a horrible machine. He was full of needles. He looked so sad, so tired. It was as if they were sapping the life out of him. And I saw a monkey act like a dog!"

Suddenly, Dave's jaw dropped. *What?* This sounded kind of familiar. . . .

Of course, everyone in the courtroom was laughing, but now Dave really wanted to hear more.

"*How* did the monkey act like a dog?" Dave asked.

"It was growling . . . chasing its tail," Forrester explained. "It's true! I'm not crazy!"

The spectators in the courtroom laughed again, but Dave was practically panting. Actually, maybe he *was* panting. He approached Forrester.

"The dog you saw, what did it look like?" he asked quietly.

"It was a big, woolly sheepdog," Forrester said.

Dave's mouth went dry. This had to mean something. "No further questions, Your Honor," Dave said.

As soon as court was adjourned, Dave took off after Kozak. He needed some answers. Kozak was moving fast, though. The reporters who were outside the courtroom tried to stop Dave, and before he knew what he was doing he had barked at them. The reporters backed off, but by the time Dave got around the corner, Kozak was nowhere to be seen.

Dave's assistant caught up with him and reminded him that he was late for a parent-teacher conference. Josh's math grades had been dropping. Dave was supposed to meet Rebecca at Josh's school so they could talk to the teacher about it.

Suddenly, Dave saw his boss approaching. "Dave! What on earth is wrong with you? You just barked at reporters!" Hollister cried angrily.

"It's the food poisoning," Dave said. "Gotta go. We'll talk later."

"What kind of food poisoning makes you bark like a dog?" Hollister called after him.

Dave showed up at Josh's school late but ready to listen. He was very concerned about Josh's grades.

Unfortunately, a cat outside the window of the classroom caused a sudden change of plans. Halfway through the conference, it jumped into view, climbing a tree in the front yard of the school. Dave couldn't take his eyes off it, just playing there—teasing him.

"Up until about a month ago, Josh was one of my best math students," the teacher said. "And then, suddenly, his grades took a dip. We're just sort of . . . searching for an explanation."

"I think the problem is me," Dave said, tearing his eyes away from the cat. "I've been very pre . . . pre . . . pre . . ."

The cat was jumping around now, prancing along a lower limb of the tree. Dave practically salivated.

"Preoccupied. With work lately," Dave finished with some effort. The cat continued to play. "I'm going to do everything I can from here on in to be there for Josh," Dave said. "He's a great kid."

Rebecca smiled. The teacher smiled. Dave was relieved, knowing he had somehow said the right thing.

And then, he couldn't take it anymore. "I've got to get back to court!" he blurted as the cat batted at a butterfly.

Then he tore out of the room, leaving Rebecca and the teacher stunned.

Outside, Dave chased after the cat as fast as his two human legs would carry him. It wasn't fast enough, though. The cat dived into moving traffic, sliding under cars and coming out on the far sidewalk. Dave ran after him, his heart pounding, and ended up right in front of an Animal Control truck. The driver slammed on his brakes, but Dave barely noticed. He had to get that cat!

The cat ran under a Dumpster, and Dave got on his knees, grabbing for it with his hands. And then, before he knew what was happening, his hands had turned into paws. Dave was a sheepdog again!

"Aw, nuts!" Dave said, letting out a bark.

Then, out of nowhere, a loop of rope fell around his neck. Dave looked up to find the Animal Control worker sneering down at him. He'd been caught by the pound!

Back at the Grant and Strictland lab, the workers told Kozak that they had finally perfected the serum. They had created a medicine that would keep people young forever! Kozak was thrilled. He was going to be a billionaire!

Shaggy looked worriedly at the other animals in the lab. This was not good!

A few hours later, Dave—still a sheepdog—was locked in a cage at the dog pound. He jumped up, excited, when Carly, Josh, and Trey walked in.

"We've been looking all over for you!" Josh cried. Dave couldn't have been happier to see him, but he was also surprised that his son was wearing a football uniform. Josh had told him the games didn't start for weeks.

After they had sprung Dave from the pound, Josh took him to his football game. Dave was excited to see Josh play. He sat on the sidelines, panting happily, and waited. And waited. And waited. Finally, in the fourth quarter, the coach told Josh to get in the game. All of Josh's teammates groaned.

"It's okay, Coach. You don't have to play me," Josh said.

"What?" Dave cried. It sounded like a bark.

"Everyone plays," Coach said. "Come on."

Josh went into the game, and Dave jumped up. "Come on, Josh! Show 'em what you can do!" Dave cheered.

But out on the field, Josh looked confused. People laughed when he couldn't find his position. Then as soon as play began, Josh tripped over his own feet. He ran into his team's quarterback, got tackled, and dropped the ball. Everyone on the sidelines groaned.

"Ooh," Dave said, wincing.

Josh's teammates teased him as he left the field. Josh looked very upset, and Dave didn't get it. Josh was always talking about how much he loved football, but he certainly didn't look like he loved it.

As Dave loped home alongside Josh, a girl named Tracy rode up on her bike. She saw Josh's uniform and got very angry.

"Football? That's why you're not trying out for *Grease*?" she demanded. "You hate football!"

Huh? Dave wondered.

"I know, but my dad loves it," Josh explained sadly. "All he cares about is having a son who's a good football player. If I told him I wanted to do a musical instead, he'd, like, write me off as a son."

"Josh! That's not true! I just thought . . . I don't know what I thought," Dave said, feeling horrible. He knew Josh couldn't understand his barks and that just made him feel worse. It seemed like he didn't know what was going on in his son's life.

"Josh, eventually your dad is going to realize you stink and you hate it," Tracy said.

"Not if he makes me quit before he sees a game," Josh said.

Now Dave was *really* confused.

"He told me I can only play if I keep my grades up, so I started flunking math," Josh explained.

"Nooo!" Dave wailed. But a loud howl was all that came out. This was ridiculous. He couldn't believe Josh was flunking math just so Dave would let him quit football. He really *didn't* know what was going on in his son's life!

Back at the Douglases' house, Carly and Trey were hanging out in Carly's room, looking at a pamphlet Carly had made for her animal-rights group.

"This is great, Carly. You rock," Trey said.

Just then, Dave came in and nudged the pamphlet with his dog nose.

"This is really well done," he said. "Carly, you did this?"

"Aren't you glad you didn't get that tattoo now, though?" Trey asked. "I mean, after Forrester's testimony? He made the whole movement look ridiculous."

"One thing I learned from Mr. Forrester is that just because something seems ridiculous doesn't mean it's wrong," Carly said. "It just takes more courage to stand up for it."

Dave was impressed. "Wow. You really are committed to this, aren't you?" he said. "I'm so proud of you, sweetheart!" Unfortunately, once again, the only thing that came out was barking.

"I mean, just imagine what would have happened to Shaggy if we hadn't stolen him from Grant and Strictland," Carly said, petting Dave's head.

"*You what!?*" Dave cried.

But Carly chose that moment to toss Dave out of her room and close the door.

Just then Josh came down the hall. "Let's order some pizza!" he cried, pounding on his sister's door. "Mom and Dad are out to dinner!"

Dave's heart nearly stopped. Dinner! He was supposed to be having a big, romantic anniversary dinner with Rebecca right now! She was going to be *so* mad!

Dave ran to his and Rebecca's special restaurant, stealing a bouquet of roses from a street vendor and clutching them in his teeth. He got to the restaurant and put his front paws up on the window. There was Rebecca, sitting at their usual table, looking sad.

I'm a dog. I can't go in there, Dave realized, his spirits falling. I'm so sorry, honey.

Rebecca looked up and saw the sheepdog at the window. Her jaw dropped. "Shaggy!?"

Five minutes later, Dave was sitting in the passenger seat of Rebecca's car as she sped home.

"I can't believe this," she shouted into her cell phone, leaving a message for Dave. "First, you completely ignore me, and now you send the *dog* with *roses* in his mouth? Are you *trying* to push me away?"

Rebecca started to cry, and Dave felt awful. "No! Honey! Don't cry," he said. But all that came out was a whimper.

"Shaggy! Don't *you* cry," Rebecca said. She stopped at a red light and hugged him. "Is this how it ends? With him who-knows-where and me hugging a dog?" Rebecca asked.

"No!" Dave cried. "I'll be a better man! I promise! I love you!"

Come on, he thought. Understand me!

"I love you!" he tried again. Three words, three barks.

Rebecca stared at him. Maybe she got it! Maybe she understood!

Then she blinked and started driving again. "Don't pee in the car," she said. "We're almost home, okay?"

So much for that, Dave thought.

Back home, Dave went to sleep in the garage and once again woke up as a human. He wrote Rebecca a note and left the house in the middle of the night, hoping that he would find an answer before it was too late. He had to make everything up to his family. He knew now that Forrester was right. If Shaggy had come from Grant and Strictland, then clearly there was some freaky testing going on in their labs. Unfortunately, Forrester had decided to plead guilty. Carly's teacher was going to go to jail if Dave didn't do something fast.

So, Dave went to Grant and Strictland to try and get to the bottom of things. He used his doglike smelling skills to sniff the walls of the building until he found an air vent. The moment he smelled the air, he knew there were animals inside the building. Forrester had been telling the truth all along!

Dave could tell he was never going to fit through the vent, but he had an idea. If he was his Shaggy self, he could definitely get through. But could he make himself change? He decided to give it a try. He grabbed a stick and ran up to a homeless man who was walking by.

"Hey, buddy! Will you throw this stick as far as you can?" Dave asked.

Looking a little confused, the man threw the stick, and Dave took off after it. He ran and ran and ran. His heart pounded. His tongue hung out. And by the time he caught up with the stick, Dave was a dog again!

"Wow! I can't believe that worked!" Dave exclaimed.

He ran back to Grant and Strictland and squeezed into the vent.

Inside the lab, the aging Strictland waited excitedly as Kozak prepared the fountain-of-youth serum. Just as Dave scurried to the lab's overhead vent and looked out, Kozak sank a needle into Strictland's arm. But instead of growing stronger, Strictland suddenly became paralyzed. His eyes stared straight ahead, and his arms froze.

"The serum doesn't work!" Gwen cried.

"Of course it works," Kozak said. "I just didn't give it to him."

The lab workers stared, confused. Up above, Dave's tongue hung out as he panted, taking in the scene. Kozak leaned close to Strictland's ear.

"Sorry to do this to you, Lance," he said. "But I couldn't let you take all the credit for my work again."

Omigosh! Dave thought. Kozak is the bad guy! Forrester was right!

"Is he dead?" Gwen asked.

"No. He's fully conscious, but unable to move or speak," Kozak said matter-of-factly. "The drug will wear off in a few months, but by then I'll be CEO and unimaginably wealthy." He threw his head back to let out an evil laugh, and at that exact moment a drop of saliva fell from Dave's tongue and dropped right into Kozak's mouth!

Kozak gagged and then spotted the sheepdog in the vent.

"Uh-oh," Dave said as he turned and raced down the air vent. Kozak ran for the elevator, but he wasn't fast enough. Dave got outside and took off on his four legs.

Back at the lab, Kozak and his workers checked the security video. They stared, dumbfounded, at the tape, which showed Dave chasing the stick and turning into a dog.

"If word of this gets out, we'll be ruined!" Kozak shouted, as he destroyed the tape. His eyes narrowed in an evil way. "Okay. Here's what we're going to do. . . ."

Dave ran straight home. He had witnessed a crime. Now he knew that Forrester was innocent and was about to go to jail for a crime he didn't commit. Somehow, he had to get his kids' attention.

But when he got home, Carly and Josh had other things on their minds. They were talking about their parents splitting up!

"Dad didn't even come home last night," Carly said. "But if you ask me, he stopped caring a long time before that."

"*No! No! No!*" Dave wailed, barking like crazy. This was the last straw. He had to tell Carly and Josh that he did care about them. He had to make them understand.

Dave spotted the Scrabble game, now on the top shelf. He sprinted across the room, leaped on the couch, jumped on the arm of the chair, and flew through the air, nudging the game down with his nose. Scrabble tiles fell everywhere.

"Shaggy!" Carly scolded.

This time, Dave got to work before his kids had a chance to clean up. He used the tiles to spell out I AM DAD.

Carly stopped in her tracks when she saw it. "That's impossible," she said, looking scared.

Dave shook his head "no." Then he spelled out: GRANT AND STRICTLAND.

Carly's eyes widened. "Forrester says they created mutant animals. And that's where I found Shaggy . . . and Shaggy bit Dad!" She dropped to her knees and hugged the dog. "Oh, Daddy!"

Dave wagged his tail. He had never felt so relieved in his life.

"So you saw the game yesterday?" Josh asked.

Dave nodded. Then he spotted the play's script. He picked it up in his mouth and brought it to his son.

Josh knew exactly what his dad meant. He could give up football and try out for the play instead. "Thanks, Dad," he said with a smile.

The reunion was interrupted when Dave's doggy hearing suddenly picked up something strange outside. He ran out to the front lawn and got the shock of his life. His legs froze. He couldn't move. He fell over on his side, tongue hanging out, and looked up and saw . . . Kozak's lab workers, holding an electric cattle prod.

"Hello there, Mr. Douglas," Larry said.

Then, he and Gwen picked Dave up and tossed him into the back of their car before Josh and Carly could do anything about it.

"Dad! Daddy!" they yelled, chasing after the car.

"Don't worry, kids! I'll be okay!" Dave shouted, letting out a few barks. "I think," he added quietly.

At the Grant and Strictland laboratory, Kozak locked Dave in a cage, right next to Shaggy, the Tibetan sheepdog.

"I'm sorry you're a dog. I'm also *very* sorry you won't be leaving here alive," Kozak told Dave. "Before you die, though, we'd like to run some tests and try to figure out just how *you* turned into *him*," he said, pointing at Shaggy.

Kozak teasingly waved his finger into the cage, and Dave instinctively snapped his jaws at him, nipping his finger.

"Ow!" Kozak shouted. "We're going to work on that attitude when I get back." Then he stormed out of the lab, leaving Dave alone with the other animals.

"Who are you and why did you bite me?" Dave barked at Shaggy.

The dog and all the other animals barked back at Dave, asking him to help them.

"How can I help you if I'm a *dog*?" he shouted back.

Shaggy suggested that he try turning back into a human. Dave told Shaggy that he always turned back when he was asleep, but he had no idea how it happened. Then Dave realized that his heart slowed down when he slept. Maybe he just needed to slow his heart down.

Suddenly, Shaggy sat up on his hind legs and began meditating. It was, after all, one of his favorite things to do.

Dave gave it a try himself. He relaxed and chanted, and all the other animals joined in. After a few minutes Dave suddenly, *finally*, turned back into a human! And he was way too big for his cage.

While Carly and Josh got Trey to drive them to Grant and Strictland to save their father, Dave managed to break out of his cage. He let all the other animals out, including Shaggy, and hoisted them into the air vents overhead so they could escape. He was just about to run out the door and meet them all outside, when suddenly, he got the second-biggest shock of his life.

Once again, Dave had been hit with the cattle prod. His arms and legs stiffened and he fell over with a thud.

Outside, the animals realized that Dave wasn't with them. They barked at Shaggy, who was sprinting away, to come back. But just then Trey's car skidded to a stop and Carly and Josh grabbed Shaggy, thinking he was Dave. "We won't let them get away with it! Don't worry, Daddy!" Carly cried. Trey sped away from Grant and Strictland, not knowing they were leaving Dave behind. All poor Shaggy could say was "woof."

Dave—still human—was thrown back in the cage at the lab. The lab workers set up a scary-looking machine for tests. They were just approaching his cage when Dave saw his friend the monkey shimmy out of the air vent behind them.

"You guys can't get away with this. You know that, right?" Dave told Gwen and Larry.

The workers smiled evilly and at that exact moment, the monkey lifted the cattle prod and knocked them both out. He raised the prod in triumph.

"Nice job, monkey!" Dave cheered.

Meanwhile, Carly, Josh, Trey, and Shaggy burst in on Rebecca at work. Carly explained everything, including the fact that her dad was now the dog sitting next to her on the floor.

"Carly, that's impossible," Rebecca said.

"The computer!" Carly cried. "C'mon, Dad! Type Mom a message!"

Shaggy just looked at her. He didn't know how to type.

"C'mon! Do it like you did at home!" Josh pleaded.

Just then, Rebecca's phone rang and she answered it. "It's your father," she told the kids.

Carly and Josh looked at Shaggy, then at each other. What was going on?

"Hi. I have so many questions for you," Rebecca said into the phone. "First off, do you know why the kids just showed up at my office with Shaggy and have been trying to convince me that he's you?"

Dave was behind the wheel of his car on his way to the courthouse with the animals from the lab. He was shocked when he heard this news. How did the kids get Shaggy? he wondered. Unfortunately, he didn't have time to ask questions.

"Meet me at the courthouse as soon as possible and I'll explain everything," he said, desperate. "I love you!"

Dave hung up the phone and kept driving. He had to get to the courthouse before Forrester was sentenced. His heart dropped when he saw traffic up ahead. He was never going to get there in time!

"I've got to go!" he cried, parking the car and leaving it to the other animals.

He sprinted for the courthouse. As he ran, his heart started to pound harder and harder and harder until, finally, he turned back into a sheepdog.

As a dog, Dave could run much faster. He raced for the courthouse, leaping, jumping, and running with all his might. Up ahead, he saw his family, Trey, and Shaggy on the steps outside and ran even faster. He hurtled to a stop in front of them and tried to catch his breath.

"*Slow* that heart down," he told himself.

"Dad? Is that you?" Carly asked.

Dave barked a yes.

"It can't be. He's a dog!" Rebecca exclaimed.

"Would a dog say this?" Dave asked, barking. "I love you! I love you! I love you!" He kept saying it until his barks started sounding like the words "Rai ruv roo!"

Suddenly Rebecca's eyes welled with tears. She dropped to her knees and hugged Dave around his shaggy neck. "Oh, honey! I love you, too!"

And that was all Dave's heart needed. Suddenly, he turned back into a human. Rebecca nearly fainted. Trey and Carly went wide-eyed.

"That was cool!" Josh exclaimed.

"Daddy, I'm so sorry," Carly said.

"No, I'm the one who's sorry, kiddo," he replied. "And I'm going to make it up to you, but right now, I've got a trial to stop."

Dave and his family burst into the courtroom before Forrester could enter his plea. "Hold everything!" Dave shouted. "Forrester is telling the truth! Kozak set the fire to cover up an illegal genetic-testing program!"

Kozak's jaw dropped. How did Dave get out? he wondered. Then he tried to make a break for it.

Dave knew that both his saliva and his dog bite had gotten into Kozak's system. By now, the evil doctor was going through the same changes Dave had gone through.

"Kozak! Stay!" Dave shouted. Kozak stopped in place.

"We'd like to recall Dr. Kozak to the stand," Hollister suddenly announced.

"You are on a short leash," the judge warned Dave. "This court has lost its patience for ridiculous behavior."

"Your Honor, just because something seems ridiculous doesn't mean it's wrong. It just takes a little more courage to believe in it," Dave said, smiling over at his daughter. Carly grinned back.

Dave approached Kozak on the stand. "Did you set fire to your lab to frame Justin Forrester because you needed to hide the fact that you were doing illegal genetic testing for a fountain-of-youth drug?" he asked.

"No," Kozak replied.

"And are you performing illegal tests on animals?" Dave continued.

"No," Kozak repeated.

"Yes, you did!" Dave snarled at Kozak.

"No, I didn't!" Kozak cried. And then, he growled.

"Tell us the truth!" Dave shouted. Kozak started to scratch behind his ears faster and faster. Dave growled at him. Kozak growled back.

"No more growling!" the judge cried.

"Did you inject Mr. Strictland with a debilitating serum?" Dave asked.

Kozak growled again, baring his teeth. Dave snarled in return.

"That's it, Mr. Douglas!" the judge shouted. "You're through! Bailiff, please remove Mr. Douglas from my courtroom."

"Come on, you mutt!" Dave shouted at Kozak. "Tell us the truth!"

The bailiff approached Dave. Sensing this was his last chance, Dave reached out and grabbed the bailiff's baton.

"Kozak! Fetch!" he shouted as he threw the baton as far as he could.

Kozak jumped out of his chair, bounded on all fours across the courtroom, and caught the baton in his mouth. When he stood up again, he had a long, shaggy tail wagging behind him. A few people in the court-room screamed. The judge's mouth dropped open.

"Now, if that's not evidence of genetic testing, I don't know what is," Dave said.

The judge nodded as cameras flashed. "Bailiff, take Dr. Kozak into custody."

The bailiff dragged Kozak off to jail. "You haven't seen the last of me! You don't know who you're dealing with!" Kozak shouted. "Woof! Woof! Ooh! Are we going outside?" he asked excitedly.

Outside the courthouse, moments after Mr. Forrester was declared innocent, Hollister approached Dave. "You got this one right, after all, and this is just the kind of exposure you need to get elected district attorney."

Dave looked around at the reporters and journalists waiting to speak with him. "Not right now, Ken. I've got more important people to talk to," he said.

And with that, he walked over to his family.

"You did it! You're my hero!" Carly exclaimed, hugging her dad.

"You don't know how good it is to hear that, kiddo," Dave said. And with that, Dave and his family—along with a new addition, a very special dog named Shaggy—headed home.